How to HELP a PUMPKIN GROW

Ashley Wolff

BEACH LANE BOOKS

New York London Toronto Sydney New Delhi

Dig it.
Spade it.
Seeds to sow.

Keep seeds warm,
Protect from snow.

I want to help a pumpkin grow.

Fence them.
Guard them.
They're so slow!
Keep them safe from hungry crow.

You want to help a pumpkin grow?

Feed them.
Weed them.
Start to show—
leaves above and roots below.

You want to help a pumpkin grow?

Drench them.
Quench them.
Let it flow.
Watering up and down the row.

You want to help a pumpkin grow?

Twine them.
Vine them.
Watch them go,
filling up the garden—**whoa!**

You want to help a pumpkin grow?

Pick them.
Stack them.
Overflow!
Room for any others?
No!

We have helped
these pumpkins grow.

Roast them.
Toast them.
Roll out dough.
Perfect pies
all in a row.

So glad we made these pumpkins grow!

Scoop them.
Scrape them.
Carve just so.
Place them so the candles show.

Now we've made our pumpkins . . .

For Wayne Kingsley—a man outstanding in his field

BEACH LANE BOOKS

An imprint of Simon & Schuster Children's Publishing Division
1230 Avenue of the Americas, New York, New York 10020
© 2021 by Ashley Wolff
Book design by Karyn Lee © 2021 by Simon & Schuster, Inc.
All rights reserved, including the right of reproduction in whole or in part in any form.
BEACH LANE BOOKS and colophon are trademarks of Simon & Schuster, Inc.
For information about special discounts for bulk purchases, please contact Simon & Schuster Special Sales at
1-866-506-1949 or business@simonandschuster.com.
The Simon & Schuster Speakers Bureau can bring authors to your live event. For more information or
to book an event, contact the Simon & Schuster Speakers Bureau at 1-866-248-3049 or visit our website at
www.simonspeakers.com.
The text for this book was set in Freeday Sans.
The illustrations for this book were rendered in acrylic gouache on Fabriano watercolor paper.
Manufactured in China
0421 SCP
First Edition
10 9 8 7 6 5 4 3 2 1
CIP data for this book is available from the Library of Congress.
ISBN 9781481419345
ISBN 9781481419352 (eBook)